Sumsy
and the Sunflower

Illustrations by Craig Cameron

EGMONT

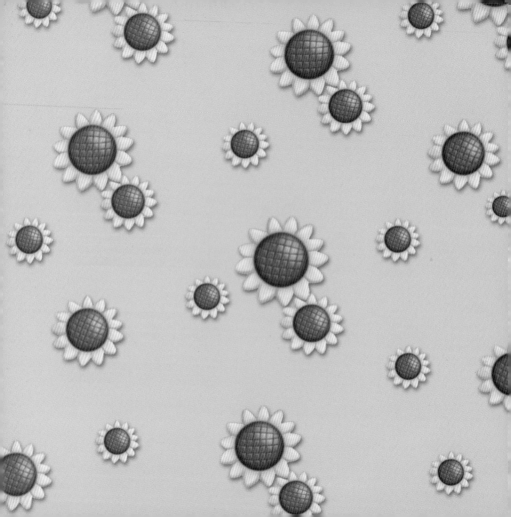

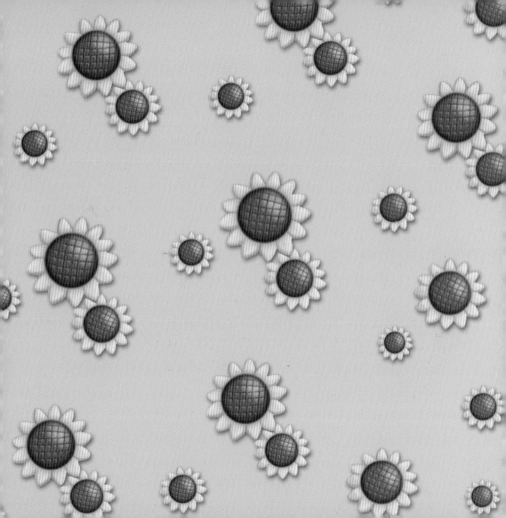

EGMONT

We bring stories to life

First published in Great Britain 2008
This edition published in 2010
by Egmont UK Limited,
239 Kensington High Street, London W8 6SA
Endpapers and introductory illustrations by Craig Cameron.

ISBN 978 1 4052 3747 5

1 3 5 7 9 10 8 6 4 2

Printed in Malaysia

Farmer Pickles' Sunflower Oil Factory is almost ready to open! There's just one more job to do. Sumsy arrives to help, but will the factory open on time?

Farmer Pickles was getting ready for the grand opening of his new Sunflower Oil Factory.

"There's just one more job to do," he said. "I need somewhere for all these boxes."

"No problem," smiled Bob. "We'll build you a bottle depot."

"Thanks, Bob," said Farmer Pickles. "Now I've got a surprise for you! Meet . . ."

"Sumsy the forklift! She's going to move the boxes with the bottles of sunflower oil from the factory to the storage depot."

"I can pack 'em! I can stack 'em!" smiled Sumsy. "Hi, everyone!"

"Hello, Sumsy," said Bob, Scoop and Travis.

She looked at Travis. "One, two, three boxes. I love counting!" Sumsy laughed.

"Right!" said Bob. "I'd better get started building this depot." And off he went.

Farmer Pickles and Travis went too, and Scoop and Sumsy were left on their own.

"I'm Scoop!" said Scoop. "I know everything about Sunflower Valley. I'll show you around. Follow me!"

"What about the boxes?" Sumsy worried. But Scoop had rolled away.

The first stop on Scoop's tour was the homestead. Then he showed Sumsy the workshops and the storerooms. "We've plenty of time to work," said Scoop.

But Sumsy looked sad. She knew there were lots of boxes to be moved.

Soon, they reached the site where Bob and the team were building the bottle depot.

"Hi, Scoop!" smiled Dizzy.

"Hi, everyone," called Scoop. "This is Sumsy! Sumsy, meet Dizzy, Muck and . . . Roley."

"Rock and ro-ho-ole!" said Roley.

"Three machines. Three!" counted Sumsy. "Three boxes is how many I can fit on my forklift. I can pack 'em, I can stack 'em!" she laughed, and raced away.

Just then, Farmer Pickles arrived with a big crate. "Look what I've got here!" he said. "A bottle-labelling machine."

He pressed a button and labels began to fly out, sticking themselves to Dizzy, Roley and Bob!

"We're not bottles! Ha, ha!" smiled Dizzy.

"What a sticky situation!" said Farmer Pickles. "I hope Sumsy brings those boxes of bottles soon."

Inside the factory, Sumsy was hard at work. "Coming through! Ten bottles in every box," she said, whizzing past Scoop.

"Wait!" moaned Scoop. I haven't shown you all the factory yet! How can I tell you things if you keep driving off?"

Sumsy raced away, with Scoop chasing behind.

Scoop caught up with Sumsy and swerved in front of her to make her stop.

Sumsy screeched to a halt, but it was too late. CRASH! The boxes flew off her forklift and smashed on the ground.

"Oh, no!" cried Scoop.

Sumsy and Scoop went to look at the mess. The bottles were broken and oil had spilled everywhere.

Meanwhile, Bob and the team had nearly finished building the bottle depot.

"Well done, team. We're almost ready for your bottles, Farmer Pickles," he said.

"But then we need labels on the bottles," worried Farmer Pickles. "Where's Sumsy?"

"Here she comes!" said Dizzy, as Sumsy trundled sadly towards them.

Farmer Pickles saw the boxes of broken bottles. "Oh dear!" he gasped.

"I'm sorry, Farmer Pickles," said Sumsy. "I was trying to do my job, when, erm . . ."

"It was me," said Scoop. "I got in Sumsy's way. I was showing her around the valley."

When Scoop found out that the bottles all needed labels, he felt very sorry. "There's not enough time!" he cried.

"Three boxes fit on my forklift, and two fit in your digger," Sumsy said to Scoop, kindly. "We'll work together to get the job done quicker!"

So that's what they did. Before long, all the boxes were safely in the depot and all the bottles had labels.

Bob finished building the depot wall and the factory was ready to open, just in time!

The grand opening was the next day. "I declare this Sunflower Oil Factory open!" said Farmer Pickles. And he snipped the ribbon in half.

"Hooray for Farmer Pickles!" cheered Bob.

"And hooray for Sumsy and Scoop!" said Farmer Pickles, proudly.

"Ha, ha!" laughed Sumsy. "When we work together, it's as easy as one, two, three!"

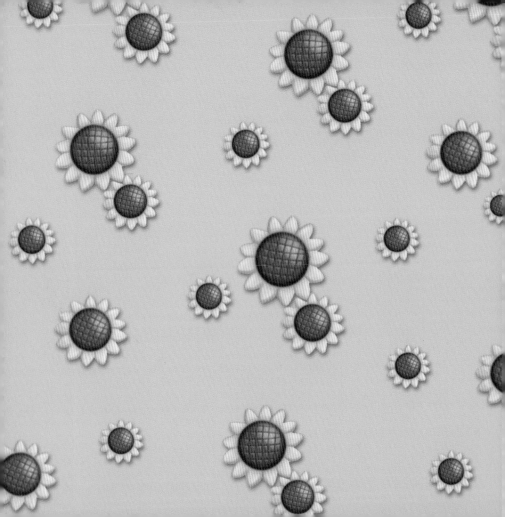

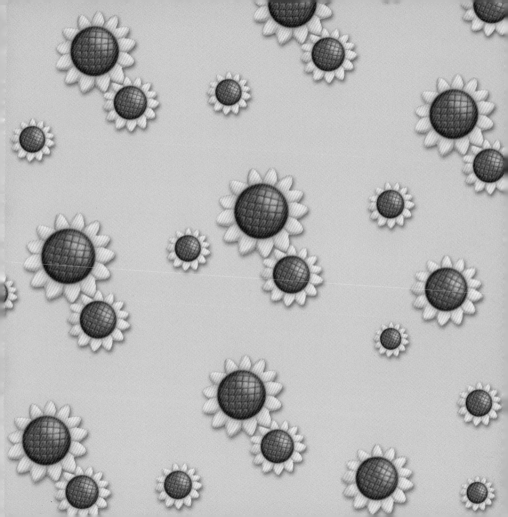